"I think these books are cool because you
actually get involved with them."
Melanie Armstrong, age 12

"I think these books are great! I really like
getting to be one of the characters."
Ahn Jacobson, age 11

"I think that this book was very exciting
and it is fun to choose your ending.
These books are great for all ages, too."
Logan Volpe, age 12

"I love the way that you can choose your own
adventure and that the author makes you
feel like you are the characters."
Shannon McDonnell, age 10

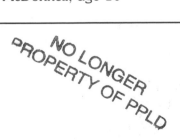

Watch for these titles coming up in the
Choose Your Own Adventure® series.

Ask your bookseller for books you have missed
or visit us at cyoa.com to learn more.

SMOKE JUMPERS

BY R.A. MONTGOMERY

ILLUSTRATED BY LAURENCE PEGUY
COVER ILLUSTRATED BY WES LOUIE

CHOOSECO
WAITSFIELD, VERMONT

Smoke Jumpers ©1991 R. A. Montgomery
Warren, Vermont. All Rights Reserved.

Artwork, design, and revised text © 2005 Chooseco LLC,
Waitsfield, Vermont. All Rights Reserved.

Cover artwork © 2009 Chooseco LLC,
Waitsfield, Vermont. All Rights Reserved.

Illustrated by: Laurence Peguy
Cover illustrated by: Wes Louie
Book design: Stacey Boyd, Big Eyedea Visual Design

For information regarding permission, write to:

CHOOSECO
P.O. Box 46
Waitsfield, Vermont 05673
www.cyoa.com

ISBN-10: 1-933390-29-8
ISBN-13: 978-1-933390-29-1

Published simultaneously in the United States and Canada

Printed in China

0 9 8 7 6 5 4 3 2 1

*Thanks to all those brave people
who protect our forests.*

BEWARE and WARNING!

This book is different from other books.

You and YOU ALONE are in charge of what happens in this story.

There are dangers, choices, adventures, and consequences. YOU must use all of your numerous talents and much of your enormous intelligence. The wrong decision could end in disaster—even death. But, don't despair. At anytime, YOU can go back and make another choice, alter the path of your story, and change its result.

You practice and study for months and are finally ready for your first parachute jump from a plane. It's part of the long process of becoming an elite smoke jumper, a fire fighter in the wilderness. But the driest spring and summer in decades means many aggressive fires. Your first jump quickly turns into your first firefighting job. In the midst of the rapidly moving blaze, you have to think fast. And move faster. If you don't do everything right, the inferno could catch up to you . . .

You've been lying awake for almost an hour when the early morning sun strikes your tent, flooding it with a golden light. Reaching up, you pull the tent flaps aside, letting in the cool morning air. You take a deep breath, the smell of pine filling your lungs. Then you tug the zipper on your sleeping bag, running it halfway down the bag.

With as much energy and enthusiasm as you can muster at this hour of the morning, you welcome the new day that lies ahead. "Rise and shine," you say. "Rise and—"

A voice from the tent next to yours interrupts you. "I already have an alarm clock, thank you."

"You know, you really know how to start the day right, Finn. Thank you. Thank you very much," you reply.

The old tent is dome-shaped and standing up straight is nearly impossible. You climb out of your down-filled sleeping bag and manage to pull on your clothes—shorts, T-shirt, and a down vest. Then you step out into the brilliant dawn, the sun cresting the range of mountains to the north. Some of them still have snow hiding in the shadowy flanks, and once again you are taken aback by the beauty of the scene. If only you could relax and enjoy yourself.

Scheduled today is your first actual training jump—the two of you have enrolled in a special jump unit assigned to combat forest fires in the mountains of the Pacific Northwest.

Turn to page 2.

"Do you think we'll really jump today?" Finn asks.

"I don't know," you say. "Weather looks good. We're ready and so are Patty, Alison, and Michael. I'd say it's a go."

Just hearing your own words once again gives you a shiver of excitement tinged with real fear. You've been through weeks of training here in the wilderness to become a smoke jumper. You have packed and repacked your chute, and practiced jumps close to the ground. You've learned to carry heavy loads of more than forty pounds for three miles in just forty-five minutes. Today may be the day: your first real parachute jump. You are ready and eager, but you are also scared. Your secret fear is that you might freeze during your first jump and your friends will see you as a coward.

Fighting fires comes later, assuming you pass the jumping tests. You try your best not to be too doubtful and focus on the importance of your newly acquired skills. You remind yourself that more than half of the training group has already dropped out due to the pressure of the job. You and Finn, your tent mate, both remain. The two of you became friends quickly because you both come from cities and have become used to camping in the wild terrain together. You are both keen environmentalists, and you've learned that smoke jumping is crucial in extreme forest fires.

Go on to the next page.

"We'd better jump. I'm getting tired of this waiting," Finn says, bringing you back to reality.

You nod in agreement and busy yourself with the details of cleaning up the tent and the campsite. The others are just emerging from their tents, and their chatter is very similar to Finn's and yours.

Turn to the next page.

4

Breakfast, as usual, is mammoth: pancakes, eggs, bacon, toast, cereal, juice, and tea. The cook, Dot Jones, grew up on a California dairy farm and became NCAA shot put champion and ten times World Women's Arm Wrestling champion. Despite her size, she's a sweet gentle soul, although you notice no one criticizes her cooking to her face.

"Dig in!" Dot urges. "You eat like birds. You're gonna be eating smoke soon, so you'd better have some real food now while you can. What's with all of you, anyway?"

You're tempted to tell her that birds actually eat more food each day than humans do in proportion to their body weight, but you resist the temptation. You don't want Dot to think you're a wiseacre. She's really very nice and always encouraging everyone, downplaying the dangers and the difficulties.

You notice the other tables in the dining hall are empty once again; the veteran jumpers are out on a fire on a fork of Bear Creek, some eighty miles from camp. They've been gone for three days, and there are reports that they're having trouble. Several times during the last few days you've thought you smelled smoke in the air. When you ask Dot, she sniffs and agrees.

"See them clouds, those dark smudgy ones?" she asks "Well, more than likely that's smoke from the fire, coming downriver from one of those steep valleys. Some say it was lit."

Go on to the next page.

"What do you mean?" you ask, knowing her answer.

"Just that. Someone set the fire. Happens, and when it does, it's nasty."

"But why? Why would someone do something like that?"

"Some folks can be strange." Dot shrugs and shakes her head. "What's important is to put them out once they start. Most fires are caused by nature. You know, lightning strikes and does its work. And when it's dry like this summer, we're in for some hot times."

As you finish your breakfast, Henry Brouillard arrives in his 4X4 pickup, a cloud of road dust kicking up behind him. Henry is in charge of the summer program. He's a native of New Orleans. As Henry likes to say, "A man raised on floods and water is bound to be attracted to drought and fire." Henry stands over six feet tall. With mahogany skin and piercing eyes, you get the feeling any fire that saw Henry coming would turn and burn in the other direction. Although Henry's tough, he's fair and truly interested in his job and the welfare of all his jumpers.

Turn to the next page.

6

Jumping down from the truck, Henry strides across the open ground, smiling and yet looking determined at the same time.

"Okay! Gather 'round, everybody. This is what you've all been waiting for. It's also what you've been dreading," he says, chuckling. There is a sprinkle of nervous laughter, but not from you. "Today, at 0900 hours, you will make your first jump. As you know, you need ten jumps to qualify as a smoke jumper."

A whoop of excitement goes up, and there is a lot of back slapping and poking in the ribs from your group of soon-to-be jumpers.

"Quiet down. Have your gear ready and meet me at the airfield, ready to go, in ten minutes."

Three hours later, you are climbing with the others up an aluminum ladder into the Otter transport plane that is used as a jump ship. As you climb aboard, the starboard engine is already ticking over and the prop wash gives everyone a good fanning. It takes a few seconds for your eyes to adjust to the dark interior of the plane. Inside, the ten of you, plus Brouillard and the no-nonsense jumpmaster Erica Hepburn, take your seats. Erica checks with the ground crew, then closes the door. Nobody is talking. They all are either staring at the floor or double-checking their gear.

Turn to page 8.

8

The plane rolls down the dirt runway and slowly lifts off, climbing into the clear morning air. You try to convince yourself that the butterflies fluttering in your stomach are from excitement, not fear.

Twenty minutes later, the plane has reached the proper altitude. It begins to circle in slow arcs, and you look out of the small rectangular window at the ground below. Everything looks so small when you are almost three thousand feet above it: trees, streams, cars, and buildings. The mountains rise all around you to the north and west. If only you could just enjoy the view and not have to worry about jumping.

Suddenly a voice cuts through your reverie. It comes from a speaker mounted on the bulkhead separating the cargo hold from the pilot's cabin, and repeats, "Approaching drop zone."

A red light winks on and off above the cargo door that is about to be your exit to the jump. Below the red light is an unlit green light. Yours are not the only eyes that are glued to these lights, waiting for your signal to jump.

Go on to the next page.

Brouillard stands up. He makes some last-minute adjustments to his equipment, tugging here and there on the harness and the webbing. Everyone else does the same.

"The first jump will be a static line jump," he instructs you. "When you step out of the plane, all you have to worry about is the position of your body. The chute will open automatically when the rip cord, attached to the line in the plane, is pulled taut."

Turn to the next page.

10

"You're about to enter an elite team of fire-fighters," Brouillard hollers over the engine. "The next time you do this, you may be suspended above a fire so out of control that peoples' lives will depend on your successful jump."

"Okay! Piece of cake. All of you will do fine!" says Erica, but her attempt to calm you down doesn't really work. Your stomach feels like it's no longer a part of your body; you can almost hear your heart beating.

Go on to the next page.

Something inside you, a premonition perhaps, tells you not to jump. It's only natural to have second thoughts, you realize. You look down again. Can you go through with it?

*If you decide to abort the jump,
turn to page 31.*

*If you decide to go ahead with the jump,
turn to page 13.*

You set aside your fears as best you can and decide to go through with the jump after all.

"Ten seconds to drop," the pilot announces. The red light then blinks off and the green light comes on.

"Everybody hooked up?" Erica asks. Everybody nods, checking to see that they are hooked up to the static line. You see Finn, and he gives you the thumbs-up signal. He looks calm, and you envy him, although he's probably feeling the same as, if not worse than, you are.

"Let's go!" Brouillard shouts. The first person steps out without hesitation, then the second, and then the third. But the fourth person hesitates, his fingers gripping the side of the fuselage. Brouillard unhooks him from the static line, and he steps aside as the rest of you continue with the jump.

Turn to the next page.

14

It's your turn, and you step out into thin air. Your stomach lurches as you begin to freefall. Your chute opens automatically with a snap and fills with air, straining against your shoulders. You hang in the air, gently falling toward the beautiful world below. Treetops are small enough to be broccoli heads and you kick your legs out to feel the resistance of the wind. The parafoil supports you. It has swelled from bunched-up, multicolored nylon into a ribbed, rectangular shape that works like the wing of a plane. It is very different from the old round parachutes. These can be directed with much greater precision, and the landing, if done right, can be gentle enough for you to hit the earth without much shock to your feet.

Your spirits are rising--you've done it! Looking out, you see the red and yellow parafoils of the others around you. A feeling of exhilaration and well-being overcomes you, but you remember what Erica and Brouillard have drummed into your head. "Be awake! Concentrate! You're not sightseeing!" Maintaining your excitement, you focus your attention on the wind and the rapidly approaching ground.

Turn to page 16.

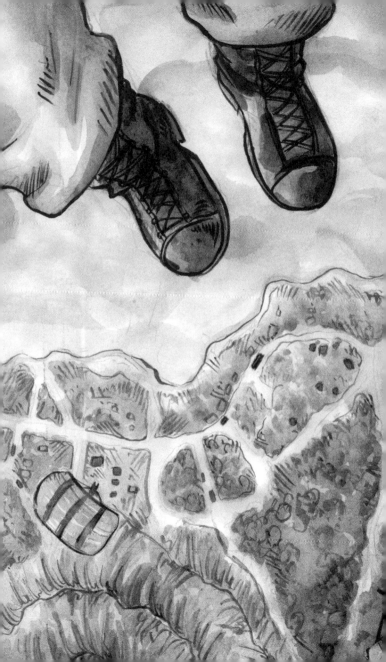

16

Erica and Brouillard were the last ones out of the plane, but they were in freefall long enough to catch up with the rest of you. You see them hanging from their chutes, and they give you a thumbs up.

Two assistant jumpmasters are on the ground with battery-powered bullhorns. They are giving directions and encouragement "Watch the wind. Hey, you, more to the right! Good job, all of you. You're doing just fine."

You watch as the first two jumpers touch ground. The first one does it textbook style, stepping down, her chute emptied of air. The second is not as fortunate. He hits the ground hard and tumbles, being dragged a few yards before his chute spills its air. An assistant jumpmaster quickly goes to his aid. You take a deep breath and hope you land safely on your own.

Turn to page 18.

Now it's your turn! The ground comes up fast. Instinctively you adjust the risers the way you have practiced. You feel a small jolt, like coming off a chairlift, and you are on the ground and standing. The others follow. Almost evenly they are divided between those who take a tumble and those who don't. No one is hurt.

You watch as Erica and Brouillard land. You are so excited with your accomplishment that you want to climb right back into the jump plane and do it again.

"Well done, all of you!" Brouillard says as he goes from person to person, shaking hands and slapping backs. "Congratulations, you're all jumpers now."

You sit down in a circle to discuss the success of the jump.

"You've all done extremely well," Erica continues for Brouillard, "but there's still a lot left to learn. Each area you jump will be different, and today there was no fire—no peril, no risk. We can learn a lot in this area nonetheless."

Erica tells you about the area of the mountains you're in now, and what makes them particularly vulnerable.

Go on to the next page.

"I made my first smoke jump not far from here," she tells you, "the Bear Jaw Fire of 1995. We lost an entire face of the San Francisco Peaks."

Another trainee named Sally raises her hand. "Wasn't that the fire where the mysterious Indians came out of nowhere to fight the fire?"

Erica looks momentarily uneasy. She glances at Brouillard and continues, "Many locals helped but there's no mystery about it. It's classic good firefighting."

Turn to the next page.

You find that it is difficult to concentrate fully on what Erica and Brouillard are saying. You know that you should pay attention, but the excitement of the day obscures their words. Your mind drifts back to the incredible feeling of being in the air, being a part of it, moving slowly toward earth and being able to control your path as if you were flying.

Erica is talking about the dangers of dropping into a fire zone. She mentions the rising air currents, called thermals, and explains how difficult they are to judge.

In the midst of this talk, Brouillard gets a call on his radio and leaves for a second, returning breathless. "I need two volunteers," he announces in a measured but excited tone. All attention is focused on him instantly; even Erica is waiting on his next words.

"We've got a problem," Brouillard says. "About sixty miles northwest of here there are a couple of small fires, nothing big. Local groups should have them under control soon, but you can't bet on that. We've got to check the situation out. As you know, our other regulars are on that big burn up on Bear Creek. I need two volunteers to come with me. Any takers?"

Go on to the next page.

Everyone's hand shoots up. Brouillard surveys the group, pleased with the response. "There is a downside to this mission," he continues. "Whoever goes will miss two or three days of jump training. We'll do our best, but you'll be missing time, and all of you know the rules. To qualify, you have to complete all the jumps. Unfortunately this will delay your certification as a smoke jumper until we can reschedule the jumps you missed. Any takers still?"

The opportunity is certainly an exciting one, but you're not sure if you want to delay your certification. After all, that's what you've been working for. The more you think about it, however, the more you realize that the bottom line in your decision to train is to put out fires and save lives. And this is your chance. Rescheduling the jumps wouldn't be the worst thing that could happen to you. The experience you would gain from going on this fire could only be valuable and would certainly look good on your record.

If you decide to volunteer and go with Brouillard, turn to page 22.

If you decide to stay with the jump class, turn to page 45.

"I'll go, Chief," you say, somewhat surprised by your own conviction.

"Me too," Finn shouts, standing up. The others seem relieved that there are enough volunteers. They remain silent, turning their attention back to Erica's instruction and the problems of landing in a burn zone.

"Okay, follow me," Brouillard says. "And thanks. I appreciate what you've given up. I'll do my best to make it up to you."

Moments later the three of you are bouncing along a dirt road in a 4X4, headed to a helipad where the two Alouette helicopters are parked. This is the first time you've ever been inside one of these French jet helicopters, well known for their ability to perform at high altitudes in the Alps of Europe. Quickly you load your gear into the far one. With Brouillard at the controls, you lift off the pad, swerve into the air like a dragonfly, heading for the site of the first fire.

You feel like a veteran now that you have had your first successful jump, but you don't want to get too sure of yourself. Jumping is dangerous, just like riding a motorcycle or climbing mountains. You are risking your life. You must take nothing for granted. Be prepared and concentrate, you remind yourself among the noise of the rotors.

Turn to the next page.

The scenery below speeds past. Thirty-five minutes later, you circle a patch of smoke. Brouillard points to it, nods his head, and searches for a landing area. He spots one, a break in the trees cut just for this purpose, over by two people signaling with a yellow groundsheet. The Alouette descends swiftly.

When the rotors come to rest, the three of you climb out. You smell freshly cut pine and wood smoke. The two smells bring back memories of camping trips with your dad when you were younger. He always took you and your sister up into northern Canada to canoe and fish for two weeks every summer, from the year you were seven until you were fourteen. That last summer was the best. You caught a salmon that was record size—at least in your family—and it was exciting enough to dilute the unhappiness of your parents' divorce. It felt really good being out in the woods and lakes, and you had a lot of fun. Even though you loved your friends in the city you grew up in, the time you spent outside with your family together in the wilderness is what you always remember as the best parts of the year. That's what families are all about, you've always thought: enjoying each others' company, sticking together, and no fighting. That was one of your dad's rules. Arguments were okay, he would always say, but fighting was out; he wouldn't tolerate it. You realize your mind is wandering and you need to focus on the mission ahead of you.

Go on to the next page.

"Hey! You okay?" Brouillard asks, coming up to you with a quizzical look.

"Yeah, I'm fine," you say. "Smoke got to me for a moment. I guess I'm still a little excited from the jump."

"Well, come on over. I want to introduce you to these guys," Brouillard says. Finn, you notice, has already walked over and introduced himself.

Before you get a chance to shake hands with the two rangers, you are interrupted by the sound of the walkie-talkie, hanging from the limb of a pine in the clearing.

"Ranger Three! Ranger Three! Mayday! Need a medevac upriver. Do you read?"

"Loud and clear. Standing by," Ranger Three replies.

"There's a ranger down. Looks like smoke inhalation. We need Brouillard and his chopper. Our other one's out."

Brouillard nods assent.

"He's on his way. He'll meet you at base camp over by Rocky Ridge."

"Negative. Further upstream. Tell him to be careful. It's gonna be tight getting in. We need help fast. Vital signs are weak."

Turn to page 27.

Before the message is completed, Brouillard is already at the helicopter. Moments later, he is airborne and away.

You stare at the quickly receding copter, wondering what is next. But you don't have to wonder for long. The ranger finishes up with his message on the radio and turns toward you and Finn.

"Name's Stamos," he says to you, introducing himself. "I've got to send a patrol out along that rim," he continues, pointing to the distant horizon and getting down to business. "We've had a report that there might be some campers over there. If this fire spreads, it could be bad. I also need help with the fire we've got going right here. It's almost under control, but our rangers need a break. We could use some new blood."

You've gone from first jump to firefighting and patrols all in the same day. You've always been the kind of person who can accept change and to be flexible in developing situations, but you think you might be stepping in over your head here. You're not scared; it's just that things are moving fast, almost too fast. You look at Finn.

If you decide to go on patrol, turn to page 28.

If you decide to help the rangers with the fire, turn to page 37.

28

You decide to go on patrol and warn the campers who might be up on the rim. Stamos briefs you on the area, providing you with a topographic map. He circles an area of about four miles where the group of campers were last seen. He also gives you a radio, but he cautions you, "The range on this thing is limited. It's an old model and the batteries are weak. You can't really rely on it. Stay out of trouble. Have you got rations?"

"Well, not really. I have enough for today, I guess. A sandwich, a candy bar, a couple of oranges."

"What about a canteen? Have you got a parka or a poncho?" he asks.

You shake your head.

"Here, take this. It's the only one I have." Stamos hands you a windbreaker. It's forest green, a color that blends in too well with your surroundings. If you were in trouble out in the woods or the mountains, you might never be spotted. Your dad always stressed the importance of using bright colors in the outdoors. He said it was an extra margin of safety, and you never knew when it would be needed. You hesitate grabbing the jacket, but given the circumstances it will have to do.

Go on to the next page.

"Are you familiar with the area?" asks Stamos.

"I've been here for about a month, but only at the campsite training with the other jumpers."

Stamos nods. "I see. Well, you'll need to watch out for snakes," he said, "but I'm sure you know that. There's a lot of things to be careful of out here," he warns. "Wolves, bears, a few unfriendly people." He gives you a quick glance. "Just get the job done and head right back, and if you run into anyone that looks like they live out here, don't start anything. People are sort of territorial out here.

"You can use this canteen. Remember, sunset is close to eight o'clock. It's almost one right now. Try to get back before dark, okay? We'll meet you here," Stamos instructs.

Turn to the next page.

30

"No problem," you reply, anxious to get on your way. You can't believe the time. It seems like a week has passed since you got up this morning. Looking around, you realize Finn has already left with the other ranger to help with the fire.

"Oh, almost forgot. You got a flashlight?" Stamos asks. As anxious as he is to be on his way, you can sense that he is a careful man.

"Sure thing. It's small, but good," you reply, patting your side. Whether you're in the city or camping, you've always taken it along.

"Good luck. Stay calm. Radio me if you need to. Remember, don't take any risks. And if you see any sign of fire, beat it. Get yourself right back here, okay?"

"You can be sure of it," you reply.

Stamos flashes you a half-grin then heads off for the fire.

Turn to page 32.

You decide to listen to your inner voice and give in to your fears: With the courage of your own convictions, you unhook yourself from the static line and move over to Brouillard.

"I can't jump," you say, feeling shame and fear flush your face.

"That's okay. It happens to lots of people. Nothing to be ashamed of. Sit here," he says, moving over a little so you can sit next to him.

No one says anything, the roar of the engine filling the void. You're feeling embarrassed, but everything is going to be all right, you tell yourself.

"Okay, jumpers, get ready," Erica says, standing up and moving over to the open cargo door. The green light is on, and one by one the others move to the opening, as if in a trance, and jump. You watch as they fall, their parachutes opening swiftly and colorfully.

Obeying some command coming from deep within you, you stand, reaching up and hooking yourself back onto the static line.

The next thing you know you are at the cargo door. Without another moment of hesitation, you jump, feeling yourself freefalling. Your chute opens, and you gracefully approach the earth, enjoying the thrill of the jump and the beauty of the view that surrounds you.

The End

Taking a deep breath, you try to reach down within yourself and come up with a sense of calm and well-being. You imagine a still forest pond; it's a trick your dad taught you. You think of the pond—its calmness, its depth, and its beauty. Focusing, you see almost no ripples. You hear no sound. Your heart steadies its beat and slows down. Your mind clears, and your thoughts are focused.

Above you, the afternoon clouds have moved into their usual position. The wind picks up a bit. That could mean trouble. The wind not only feeds the fires but also carries them along. You'll have to keep the direction of the wind in mind as you patrol.

The route on the topo map is pretty straight-forward. You follow a stream for almost a mile, finding the trail easily. The trees are old and well spaced. There isn't too much underbrush. As you walk, you find it a kind of relief to be on your own, away from the excitement of the jump school and the noise of the others. You relax as your breathing settles down into its natural rhythm.

A mile or so later the stream hooks left, and you start to head uphill. The terrain is more difficult and you slip a few times. You study the map several times, making sure you're reading it correctly. You keep worrying you're getting off track. Glancing around, you realize that you also get the feeling you're being followed. Stop being so anxious, you tell yourself, these fears are just in your mind.

Turn to page 34.

Stamos has circled an area on the map marked with craggy rocks that overlook a valley and a stream. You're certain you've gone the wrong way—there are craggy rocks all right, but all you see beyond them are more craggy rocks, dry as desert. You look out over the barren land in worry. You wonder if the map is outdated, or if you've gone the wrong way. You sit for a second. I'll eat some lunch, you think, get my mind going again.

As you sit to eat, you hear a stick break. You realize your intuition was right—you definitely have not been hiking alone.

Turn to page 72.

"I don't know what to do," you reply. "I'm sorry."

"I sense that you are not who we were looking for to help us," says the medicine man. He looks at Nascha and says something to her that you don't understand.

"I think you'd better leave," she tells you. "Now!"

Turn to the next page.

"But I'm on fire watch," you argue, "I have to send in my position." From the medicine man's expression you can see that argument carries no weight. The group watches as you duck into the forest, heading away from the looming fire.

Two weeks later, you finally spot the familiar ranger uniforms as you are found, barely alive from wandering for so long, eating only strange plants you have gathered.

"Where have you been?" asks Stamos anxiously.

You look at him weakly. You remember nothing.

The End

Deciding to fight the fire, you surprise Finn by the way you speak right up.

"We'll fight the fire," you offer. He just sort of shrugs his shoulders. You hope you didn't hurt his feelings, but when you feel something's right, you go for it.

Stamos radios the firefighting team. "This is Stamos. Send Maria to patrol the ridge for pilgrims. I'm going to the fire with two of the new trainees. Over."

"Sure thing, chief, 10-4."

Turn to the next page.

"What are pilgrims?" you ask Stamos.

Stamos laughs. "Oh, just a nickname we have for campers. Nothing bad really, it's just that they're so earnest, so many seeing this country for the first time. Anyway, let's head out. Time's a-wastin'."

You pile into the beat-up pickup with Finn and Stamos. The ride to the burn area is bumpy, and Stamos drives fast. Holding on to the stanchions of the roll bar is all you can do to keep from falling out.

Stamos looks over and sees your fearful expression. He laughs and accelerates further.

"Yee-haw!" he shouts. "It's fire-fightin' time!"

Go on to the next page.

Forty minutes later, you roll into a makeshift staging area where several other vehicles are parked. The smell of smoke is particularly heavy here, and the wind has picked up, sweeping down the narrow valley toward the fire.

"Okay," Stamos says, "you've got safety gear, helmets, goggles, fire-retardant jackets. Let me see your boots." Stamos checks them, making sure they are the kind with special insulation used for jumping and fires, which they are. "Here, you'll need these," he says, tossing shovels at you and Finn. You also take your packs, canteens, and a limited amount of food. One radio is handed out, and Finn takes it. "Remember, the two of you, don't get split up. Stay in contact with the main group at all times. Fire can be really tricky. Just be careful."

As you hit the trail, you realize it's not really a trail, but a contour that snakes around rock outcroppings, drops down to the river, crosses it, and heads up the other side. It is steep, and your footing is unsure. Stamos pushes ahead, and you and Finn do your best to keep up.

Turn to the next page.

40

Once on the ridge, you stop for a moment to rest and get your bearings.

"Hey, what's that?" Finn asks, pointing to the far ridge at what appears to be a figure.

"Looks like a person. But what's he doing?" you reply.

"He seems to be signaling. Maybe he needs help."

The figure is waving a shirt and moving back and forth within a ten- or twelve-foot space. You try to shout, but it is too far, and the noise of the stream blocks your voice from traveling. You figure that hiking to the ridge would take you about fifty minutes or so out of your way.

"What do you think, Finn? Should we investigate?"

"Well, it's not that far. But maybe we should turn this one over to Stamos."

You look around, but Stamos is out of your line of sight. You could try and catch up with him but maybe you can take the situation into your own hands and see what the man wants.

If you decide to help the man, turn to page 60.

If you catch up with Stamos, turn to page 71.

You decide to go with this mysterious woman. There is something about her that makes you trust her.

Nascha nods quickly at your decision.

"I thought you'd come with me," she says. "You'll be happy you did. Just follow me—we're going to move fast."

Nascha sweeps through the land quickly and low to the ground. At first you have a difficult time following her. You are traveling on rough terrain and not following a marked path. Soon, you realize you are mimicking her movements, low like a cat,

and it becomes easier for you. Both of you are almost running along the ridge, and she never looks back or speaks to you. You stop for a drink after about an hour.

"Look out," Nascha instructs you. You scan the ridge. The rocks here are smooth and strangely shaped, and they look prehistoric. A large bird you don't recognize glides overhead. It's as if you've stepped back in time.

Turn to the next page.

"We're about to enter a part of Miwok lands where very few other people have been," Nascha tells you. "There's a forest fire there, and a cooling-down ceremony is already in progress."

"Cooling-down ceremony?" you repeat.

"Miwok believe all fires happen for a natural reason, in response to imbalances in the world. The cooling-down ceremony attempts to restore this balance." Nascha points to a rock outcropping about a half mile up from where you stand now, just barely visible in the distance. "We won't travel more than twenty minutes from there."

Amazingly, you hardly feel tired, even though you've walked very far very quickly. You feel comfortable and at ease, Finn and Stamos and Brouillard already seeming far in the past. You follow Nascha again without any feelings of anxiety about what you will encounter next.

Turn to page 52.

Finn looks over at you questioningly; you shake your head no. After all, the main reason you enrolled in the training course was to learn how to jump. You like Brouillard and don't wish to see him stranded. If no one else volunteers, then you will. Fortunately three people speak up. Brouillard picks two, and moments later they are on their way in his 4X4.

Getting on with the class, Erica stands up on a table in the mess hall. "Okay, you jumpers. Well done! I've seen a lot of first jumps, and you were all great. Every single one of you."

There is a lot of cheering and hooting. Erica lets the roar subside before she continues. "We're going to debrief all of you. We'll do it alphabetically. Everyone outside, back to your instructors!"

Turn to page 47.

Outside, the late morning sun is intense, and the smell of pine is heavy and wonderful. You feel that every breath of air that you take is charged with life. You just can't get enough of it. Having completed your jump, you feel more powerful than you have ever felt before. Enrolling in this summer program was the best idea you ever had.

Dot has prepared a special treat for everyone in honor of the first jump. Clanging an iron triangle that hangs from the rafters of the mess hall porch, she shouts, "Come and get it!" just like in the movies. Fresh slices of blueberry pie sit waiting for you.

Turn to the next page.

The debriefing takes up most of the afternoon. Erica is a good teacher and someone to be respected in her own low-key way. The session with her speeds by, and you are surprised at how much you learn just by talking about the jump and what it felt like.

"Tomorrow we'll jump again. Take the afternoon off and get some rest tonight," she tells you.

At night, however, a storm system blows in from the west, and huge cumulus clouds build up over the mountains. Wind swoops down on the camp, and the first few drops of rain spatter into the dry earth, slamming onto the taut nylon of the tent fly. Moments later the rain stops as quickly as it began, but the wind and the lightning continue. The thunder rumbles long and hard through the mountains and valleys. You know that the wind will make the fires harder to fight, and the lightning will probably set off some new blazes. All you can do now is wait it out and check your tent to make sure the pegs are secure and the fly is set.

Lights out seems early, even though it's the old standard 10:00 P.M., or as they call it, 2200 hours. Nevertheless you can forget about sleep. You're still excited from your jump earlier in the day. The sensation of being suspended above the earth, of feeling like a species other than human, alive and free, is too much to allow you to sleep.

Suddenly, you are aware of a scratching at the tent fly. It is a faint sound, but something is definitely there.

Turn to page 50.

"Hello?" you ask, tentatively.

"Keep quiet. It's me, Finn," comes back a low whisper.

"What's up? Jump got you excited? Can't sleep either?"

"No, it's more than that. Something strange is going on here."

"The only thing strange around here is you," you reply. With that you unzip the tent flap and step out into the night. The clouds are covering the moon and stars. It's hard to see, but you can make

out Finn's shape. "So, what's up?"

"Well, you might think I'm nuts, but—" Finn stops in mid-sentence, grabs you by the arm, and pushes you behind the tent. Two figures rush by.

"See those two?" he asks. "I was up, prowling around looking for something to eat in the mess hall. Dot sometimes leaves leftovers out. That's when I saw them."

"Who?" you ask.

"You never give me a chance to finish a story."

"That's because you drone on so much. Get to your point. Who were they?"

"That's it. I never saw them around here before. But they sure looked like they knew what they wanted, and what they were doing."

Turn to page 116.

After the promised twenty minutes, Nascha leads you to a flat rock overlooking a breathtaking ravine. Several men and women in white animal skins are swaying in a circle, while a man in a decorative vest passes a smoking cornhusk to each of them.

Beyond this ceremony, the fire rages intensely. The thick smoke is quickly obscuring the gorge. You notice that animals have fled uphill. Two small deer and a large elk with a wide set of antlers stand at the edge of the circle of people, as if they are watching.

Nascha joins the circle and motions for you to as well. You are both offered pinches of something yellow from a buckskin pouch.

"Corn pollen," Nascha tells you. "Take it."

You put the pollen on your tongue and the medicine man leading the ceremony pushes some pollen against your forehead, then sprinkles some on the ground and gestures at the sky.

Turn to page 54.

You follow the medicine man's gesture toward the sky with your eyes. As you look up, lightning crackles across the smoke-darkened sky. When you look back at the medicine man, you realize that for the first time, you can understand the language he is speaking in.

"We are calling on the sons of Changing Woman, Monster Slayer, and Born for Water to help us cool down this fire," he says. "I understand you've come to help us, also."

Everyone in the circle turns their attention to you. Even the elk and deer seem to be watching and understanding.

"Will you lead our ceremony?"

If you say you will, turn to page 68.

If you refuse to lead the ceremony because you have no idea what to do, turn to page 35.

Going against your better judgment, you decide to join Finn in tracking down these people in the parachute shed, whoever they may be. The joy of the day has evaporated, and you sense danger in the air. You are afraid of what might happen.

"Follow me," Finn whispers, circling the parachute shed.

You get as low to the ground as possible, then scurry after Finn. Coming up on the side of the shed, the two of you hunker down below one of the windows, which is, unfortunately, locked. The voices coming from inside are indistinct. You can't tell how many people are in there.

Suddenly the door opens, and two people step out. They look around in the darkness, then hurry off. Holding your breath, you freeze to the spot, all muscles tensed. Finn is the same way. Gently you tap him on the arm and point to the open door.

"Shall we check inside? I think they're all gone."

"Okay. I'll go first," he replies, slipping along the wall, onto the porch, then in through the half-open doorway. You follow.

"Stop! Don't move," comes a thin voice. You stop in your tracks. A flashlight flicks on, cutting a hole in the darkness. It searches your face first, then Finn's.

"Kids. I might have known it. Well, you want to play with adults, then you'll play by the rules, all right. Get going." He points toward the door.

Turn to the next page.

56

Your instinct tells you that if you make a dash for the woods you could probably get away. But how could you leave Finn to suffer the consequences if you managed to get away and he didn't?

The moment and the opportunity pass quickly as you leave the wooded path and emerge on the landing strip next to the old Otter. It looms in the darkness like some ancient dinosaur, its head pointed up, arms outstretched, and its tail down on the earth.

"In you go," comes a command. Once inside, your hands are bound with nylon parachute cord. The two of you are then hooked to the static line, only this time without a parachute. The big radial engines tick over, then burst into life. Slowly, the plane starts down the runway.

You wish this were a nightmare, but you know it isn't. You can't believe what is happening.

"Who are you? What do you want?" you manage to ask.

Go on to the next page.

The man with the thin voice hesitates, then replies, "Let's just say we are some businessmen making an investment. The two of you will be our guarantees. I'm sure someone cares for you. Let's just see how much."

The plane lurches into the air and begins a slow circle above the camp with a radius of about two miles. Intermittently the clouds break apart, and moonlight dents the dark interior.

An hour later, with gas running low, the men grow angry and more and more frustrated. Having received no response to their demands, they hurl you and Finn out into the emptiness of the sky. You've heard Erica and Brouillard suggest haystacks and swamps as a last resort to break a fall. As the ground comes up toward you, you hope those stories were true.

The End

"I'm sorry, but I can't go with you," you say to Nascha. "I have an assignment I must complete."

"I understand," Nascha says. "Be very careful in these forests, there are more dangers here than your smoke jump training may have prepared you for."

"Hey, wait a minute. I've got an idea," you say.

"What?" she asks, already picking up her back-pack to leave.

"I've got a radio. I'll report the other fire. We can get some rangers down here immediately."

"No! No, that's not necessary. We already have several people working on it," she says.

"Hey, no problem," you reply, removing the radio and beginning to key it.

"I don't need you to call the rangers," Nascha says, taking the radio from your hand firmly with a grip that surprises you. "I told you it will be taken care of."

Go on to the next page.

"I'm sorry," she tells you, "but I can't let you call the rangers—they'll just interfere. Erica and I are good friends who have worked together before, but I don't trust just anyone to invade these forests. These are places where rangers have never been before." She studies you carefully, almost threateningly. "I need to trust that you won't call the ranger station, and I'm not sure that I can."

"Nascha," you say, "I'm training as a smoke jumper, and I take it very seriously. If there's a fire, I need to report it to the station."

She considers. "Come with me and see for yourself," she says. "If you still don't believe me, you can call your ranger station. I promise you, you'll be glad you did."

If you decide to follow Nascha,
turn to page 63.

If you decide to call in the fire right away,
turn to page 90.

"Lets investigate this guy. It's not far, and he looks like he needs help. The fire's not coming from over there. We'll be safe," you say to Finn, aware that he is hesitant. You, however, are anxious to get going. Time could be very important.

Finn shakes his head. "I don't know. Stamos said not to get separated."

"Yeah, but he meant you and me. Besides, he went ahead and left us. Hey, it is not like we're in the fire zone. Come on, let's go."

"I'm staying; you go," Finn says.

You remember how stubborn he can get, almost defiant. "Fine," you decide. "I won't be long. Tell Stamos where I am. I'll catch up with you later."

For a moment you hesitate, wondering whether or not you are doing the right thing or whether you're being foolish.

It doesn't take you long to get to the other side of the river, although the water is a little rough. Even though it's low because of the almost-drought conditions, the current is fast and the rocks are slippery. You make it, and soon you are scrambling up the other side.

Within forty minutes you reach the spot where you saw the figure, only to find nobody there.

"Hey! Yo! Hey, where are you?" you shout, only to get a faint echo in return. You are alone, you realize, and whoever it was is now gone. For the next twenty minutes, you search the area without success, feeling increasingly angry and a little foolish.

Go on to the next page.

Looking at your watch, you decide it's time for you to head back. "This is what they call a real wild-goose chase," you say out loud, your anger mounting along with the dreadful self-criticism that goes with it. "I guess Finn was right after all."

It takes you longer to get back than it did going up, but eventually you catch up with Stamos, Finn, and the others. Stamos takes you aside and you fear the worst, expecting a lecture at the very least.

"Hey, look, I appreciate what you did," Stamos says. "You took a risk, and I would have done the same. But you gotta watch out. The 'Old Coyote' will get you if you don't. I sure would like to catch that joker. Whoever he is, he's in for trouble when we find him."

Turn to the next page.

You nod in agreement. Stamos's mention of the Old Coyote makes you stop and think for a moment. You remember reading that the Indians believed that the Old Coyote was a powerful spirit, responsible for all sorts of mischief. He is both a trickster and a teacher, and the Indians saw him as a reflection of themselves. They were entertained and educated by stories of the Old Coyote, passing them down from generation to generation.

Just what did Stamos mean by mentioning the Old Coyote, you wonder. Maybe he was trying to tell you that you must see things with different eyes and prepare for the unexpected, while still remaining true to your purpose, you decide. All that behind you, however, it's time for you to move on once again. There's still a fire for you to get under control.

The End

"Fine, I'll go with you," you tell Nascha. "Lead the way."

She points off in the direction of the road ahead. Thinking back, you seem to remember a beat-up pickup parked at the far end of the road. Maybe that's Nascha's vehicle.

Nascha keeps quiet, and you wonder if she knows what she's talking about. You feel like there might not be a fire on the peak after all. Who else would be working on it if there weren't any rangers up there?

You find the walking easy, but you are nervous about what lies ahead. An idea hits you. You slow your pace and slowly turn your radio on from inside your pocket.

"Nascha," you say, "can you tell me anything else about where we're headed?"

You hope that Stamos will hear your conversation and come to your rescue. But Nascha continues walking, and says nothing. Suddenly, she turns and looks at you sharply.

Turn to the next page.

64

"I know you tried to alert your friend to this fire," Nascha tells you angrily. "And it doesn't matter. The place I am taking you to is not on your topo maps. You'd better just follow me, because otherwise you're going to be lost in a terrible fire."

"What makes you so sure you know better than the rangers? I thought you worked with Erica."

"I have," says Nascha. "And I know what some people do to Miwok lands. Every fire happens for a reason, and we're going to deal with this one in our own way."

Go on to the next page.

You're intrigued by what Nascha is saying, even though you know you're about to do something dangerous. You remember Erica's warning about this area and her saying something about Miwok, but you can't remember what it was that she said. You follow Nascha silently through the forest for fifteen minutes, behind outcroppings of rock and never following any path. You begin to get a whiff of smoke in the air. You click your radio on and off, and nothing happens. Nascha smiles at you.

"That radio will not work here," she tells you.

Oddly, you feel less afraid as you walk with her. She moves confidently, even without a path, and you find that by following close behind her, you can move quickly as well. You travel this way for nearly an hour, until the air is truly thick with smoke. You still do not see a fire.

Turn to the next page.

Finally you see reach a flat outcropping of rock and Nascha gestures out. There is a dramatic ravine, a deep, sharp gully. Across the way, a domed peak thick with evergreen trees is blazing with growing forest fire. Several Miwok are standing on the flat rock, waving sticks tied with cloths at the fire. They glare at you, and then look at Nascha questioningly.

"Fires in the forest represent imbalance in the world," Nascha tells you. "We will protect the land in our own way, without interference from the outside. After all, it is the outside that has led to so much destruction of the earth already." She motions for you to join her in the circle. "Now that you've learned to be a smoke jumper, you will learn the cooling-down ceremony of the Miwok as well."

You stand beside her.

"There's one more thing," she says. "We've reached a place that the rangers don't know about—I'm afraid you can't go back, or else you might show them the way."

The End

"I will do my best," you say. Somehow you know what to do next. The medicine man nods, smiling but silent, and you can tell you made the right choice by agreeing to help lead the ceremony. He dips two feathered sticks into water and hands them to you.

You can't tell if the smoke is getting to you or if you're going crazy, but the elk that fled from the gorge walks slowly to the center of the circle. The Miwok around you just smile. You hold the feathered prayer sticks in each hand, your eyes wide.

Turn to page 70.

70

The smoke grows much thicker, and you can't believe that no one seems to be affected by it. Down in the gorge, the fire roars and charred tree trunks smolder. You wonder vaguely why no ranger copters have spotted this fire. Maybe in just moments Stamos and Brouillard will arrive to decimate this incredible burn. The medicine man, sensing your anxiety, urges you to take a deep breath and relax.

"Just be patient," he tells you.

You take a deep breath and close your eyes. You are comforted to not look at the raging fire. When you open them, you are face-to-face with the enormous elk.

Turn to page 76.

"Let's see what Stamos says," you say to Finn. "You stay here. Keep that guy in sight. I'll go up the trail and get Stamos, okay?"

"Sure, boss," Finn says, throwing you a smart salute.

"Hey, I'm just making a suggestion."

"Well your suggestion, as you call it, sounds suspiciously like a command to me. Nature abhors a vacuum, and you just love to fill those vacuums."

"Hey, ease up. I'm sorry. I didn't mean to be bossy."

"Well you are, sometimes," Finn says, lowering his voice a notch. You can tell that the fight is over. You feel bad that you hurt his feelings. Still, you are just about to counter with the criticism that he occasionally acts and talks like a preppy snob. But reason takes over, and you say nothing. One thing has nothing to do with the other.

"So, why don't we flip for it?" you suggest, taking a coin from your pocket.

"Great. I'll take heads."

You flip the coin, watching as it spins in the air, the sun catching it for just a split second and reflecting off the silver. It hits the ground with a thunk.

"Heads. You got it," you say.

"Great, you go after Stamos, and I'll stay," he says.

"Hey, wait a minute, I thought—"

"Well, don't. I was going to stay anyway. I just don't like being bossed around and told what to do. Go."

Turn to page 86.

"Is anyone there?" you ask, your hand on the radio in case you need to call for help. You wait a second and ask again. To your surprise, a woman in rugged clothing steps from behind part of the rock wall.

"I'm sorry to sneak up on you. My name is Nascha," she says. "I've been hiking near you for a while. I keep an eye on this part of the mountainside." She looks at you questioningly. "You walk like you have something important to do."

"I'm a smoke jumper," you tell her. "Well, I'm training," you add quickly. She listens intently. "I've been working with Henry Brouillard and Erica Hepburn for the past five weeks."

"I have worked with Erica myself," Nascha says, "I met her at Bear Jaw." You remember the fire that Erica described right before you left on this mission.

"Are you a smoke jumper, too?" you ask.

"Not exactly," says Nascha. She gives you a long look. "It's an interesting life, but too dangerous for me. I live in a settling of Miwok Indians very close to here."

Turn to page 74.

"You must have come from that small fire that the rangers have been working on," Nascha says. "It's too bad they're spending so much time on that little valley fire when we've got a gorge to worry about."

"Gorge?"

"Trillion Gorge, just twenty minutes from here. I'm headed up there myself." She looks at you confidently. "We could use your help, if you've really been trained by Erica."

You feel as though Nascha knows what she's talking about, and if she is a friend of Erica's, you'd like to help her. However, you don't want to desert your mission.

"We could really use your help," Nascha insists. "Trust me, no one knows this land the way my people and I do, and this fire will burn through a very old forest if we don't take care of it."

If you go with Nascha to Trillion Gorge, turn to page 42.

If you decide to continue looking for the campers, turn to page 58.

"Come on, Finn. Let's not be heroic," you say. "Let's get Erica."

"I'll go after them," Finn says. "You get Erica." Before you can argue, he is gone.

"It's always up to me," you mumble to yourself, heading for Erica's cabin.

Erica, Dot, Brouillard, and the other instructors all live in separate log cabins built in the 1930s during the Depression by young volunteers in the Civilian Conservation Corps known as "Tree Soldiers." Everyone else lives in tents.

All the lights are out. You feel a bit foolish waking them up. It's probably just some kids messing around, but you think it's better to be safe than sorry. Everyone here knows just how important the equipment is. No one would mess around with that stuff unless they were up to no good.

You rap lightly on the old wooden door of Erica's cabin. "Erica? Hey, Erica, are you in there?" you ask. But there is no answer. You try again, to no avail. Gathering up your courage, you try the doorknob. It's unlocked, and you push gently on it. The door swings softly on its hinges. You enter, peering into the darkness, and see a light coming from under the bedroom door at the back of the cabin.

There's something odd here, you say to yourself. "Hey, Erica!" you call once again, your voice louder this time.

Turn to page 78.

76

"This fire is the remains of the time of the monsters," says a low voice. You look around—no one seems to be speaking. The elk is staring at you patiently, huge eyes shining between its four-foot span of heavy antlers. It's got to be this incredible smoke, you think. "When the monsters came," continues the voice, "the Miwok were destroyed and so were the animals they depended on for food. Only a few of the larger animals are still alive today."

"We developed these ceremonies to restore balance on Earth at dangerous times," continues the voice. "Our environment is in an out-of-balance state. These fires are a signal that things are going wrong in the world. They are caused by the things that people do, but they are formed by nature.

"Now, hold those prayer sticks and we will concentrate on restoring this balance."

Turn to page 89.

A muffled groan comes from the bedroom.

"Erica!" you shout, running across the room in three steps. The door is blocked. "It's me, Erica. It's me!" you shout, pushing against the door gently. Slowly it opens. Erica's body, you discover, is blocking the door. She's been tied to a chair, a red polka-dot bandana tied securely around her mouth. Her eyes are open, filled with both anger and fear. Within moments you have her free.

"Did you see them?" she gulps after you remove the gag.

"Yes, they're in the parachute shed."

"Good lord! Let's go."

"What happened?"

"Later—we've got to stop them." Erica is off and running. She covers ground fast, and you have trouble keeping up. Moments later, you are at the parachute shed. It is silent.

You reach out and stop Erica. "Finn's somewhere around here. He was keeping an eye on them while I went and got you. Let's find him first."

Unfortunately, you don't have an opportunity to go and look for him. A flashlight rips through the darkness, shining on Finn, who is standing in the doorway of the parachute shed.

Turn to page 80.

80

"One move and this jumper's history," a sharp voice says.

You and Erica freeze where you are. Finn stands rigidly, eyes forward. His fear is most evident.

"I don't think they know that there are two of us here," you whisper into Erica's ear. "You could melt into the shadows and get Dot and the others." Erica thinks for a moment, nods her head, and whispers back, "It's risky, but it's up to you." You know that will leave you exposed, left to deal with these creeps. There's no telling who they are or what they want.

Obviously, you don't want to remain behind. But if they don't know Erica is with you, it might be worth the risk to have her run and get help. On the other hand, perhaps you should go for help. Erica is older than you—she should be able to take care of herself and protect Finn. The longer you wait, though, the less of an option you have. Whatever your decision, you must react quickly.

If you tell Erica to go, turn to page 85.

If you decide you should go, turn to page 82.

Speed is important. You run across the open land, taking a shortcut through a stand of pine, until you finally reach the motor pool area. There are three vehicles in the lot. Two are 4X4 pickup trucks, and the third is a huge U.S. Army six-wheeler, now used to haul supplies, equipment, and firefighters.

"Keys! Where do they keep the keys?" you yell out loud with frustration. Slow down. Use your brain. *Where would you hide a key if you had to?* you ask yourself. I'd just stick it under the front seat. Yeah, that's what I'd do. No one expects anyone to steal anything out here.

Reaching under the front seat of the first 4X4, you come up with nothing other than some candy wrappers and a few straws from a fast food shake.

Rats! You move to the next 4X4. Again nothing.

"I don't want to drive that monster," you say, surveying the six-wheeler. "Oh well, here goes nothing." Your dad taught you how to drive a jeep when your feet could barely touch the pedals. It's been a long time since then, but you're sure you can still do it. What choice do you have, really?

The climb up into the cab itself is a task. But there, right in the ignition, is a key hanging, waiting for you. After turning the key to light the cab, you examine the dashboard. Sure enough, there is a manual choke. You pull it out about halfway, pump the accelerator, hold it to the floor, and then turn the key all the way.

Turn to page 96.

"I'll go, Erica. You stay here," you whisper. "I'll get Dot, and we'll radio Brouillard for help."

"Listen, get the others—Patty, Alison, and Michael. Tell them to surround the shed. And send someone to the plane. Hurry."

You slink off into the woods as quietly as possible, making a beeline for the cabins. This time you don't hesitate. You knock on the door of Dot's cabin and enter without waiting.

She's not there. A quick check shows that her bed hasn't been slept in.

Maybe she has the night off, you speculate. You don't think much of it at first; however, it is a long way into town, you realize, and there isn't much there: two restaurants, a general store, one gas station, and a post office. Hardly worth calling it a town at all, but when you live out in the woods for a long stretch, anything begins to seem more and more like a city than a bump in the road, you reason.

You go on to Michael's cabin, but he's not in, either. The same with Patty and Alison. Maybe

they're all out together, you think. Then an awful thought pops into your mind, one you'd rather not think of. What if these people are all in on this together?

Turn to the next page.

84

But what in the world could their reasons be? What would be in it for them? You do your best to erase these thoughts. They couldn't be involved. Screwing around with those parachutes would be murder. Then suddenly it hits you with a double blow—you could have been murdered! The image of your chute failing to open is too graphic and too awesome for you to dwell on. You shudder at the thought.

Turn to page 95.

You decide to take the risk. Erica agrees and goes for help.

"Hey, Finn, it's me. I'm all alone," you call out, your voice tinny.

"Okay, kid," says another voice, harsh and scratchy, which you don't recognize. "Come over here. Keep your hands away from your body where I can see them. There is a rifle trained on you."

You're lucky--they haven't realized that Erica has slipped away.

Fear invades every single molecule of your body, gripping your throat like a wrench, almost choking you. Gingerly, you step forward. You feel as if the ground beneath your feet will crack like glass as you move forward, stepping into the unknown terror.

"Stay back!" Finn shouts at you. "These guys are killers."

You watch as Finn is knocked down by a vicious blow to the head. Instinctively, you dive for cover. Three bullets slice the air, thudding into the ground where you were standing just moments before. You scramble around the parachute shed, but before you can make it to the woods for safety, a stab of light catches you. You're caught!

"Don't you dare move another inch."

Turn to page 115.

Not fifteen minutes up the trail, you get into a zone of heavy smoke. Eyes stinging, nostrils clogging, you cough and hack, wondering how you'll be able to keep moving further on. You didn't expect it to be this bad. For a few moments you consider turning back, but then from out of the smoke comes Stamos.

"Hey! Where were you guys? I turned around and you were gone. Come, we need help. This fire is nastier than we thought."

"Yeah, but—"

"No time for buts, let's move it! Where's Finn?"

"He's back about a quarter mile. We saw—."

Stamos cuts you off again. "Well, get him!"

"Stamos, will you listen for a minute?" Your voice is firm, and you finally get his attention.

"Okay, what is it?"

"As I was trying to say, we saw a man back on the opposite ridge. He was waving a shirt or something. We think he needs help."

"Why didn't you tell me?"

"I've been trying to, Stamos." You are beginning to lose patience with this man. "What should we do?"

"I'll call Brouillard with the copter, let me grab another ranger." With that he melts back into the smoke as though he were an apparition.

Turn to page 88.

88

You walk back down the trail. When you find Finn, the two of you rush through the smoke to the area where the man was spotted. It's clearer here, but across the way you can see that the fire has made a turn and is approaching from both directions! You can also make out that more than one figure is standing there—about to be engulfed by flames. You radio Stamos, but there is no reply.

You try Brouillard, and hear the same static.

"I'm going to climb the ridge," Finn announces authoritatively. "You can keep waiting for them if you want."

You hesitate. You don't have any real fire-fighting experience yet. Finn doesn't even look back to see if you're following or not, but you know that even if you can't rescue the people who are stranded, you can't leave Finn on his own, either.

Turn to page 92.

The next time you open your eyes, it's twilight. You hear a noise and look behind you. The helicopters have finally arrived, and Brouillard is climbing out, Stamos and Erica behind him. Finn is already at your side.

"I can't believe we found you up here!" says Finn. "It's been hours since you wandered off."

You blink slowly and cough. Your lungs are still affected by the heavy smoke you breathed in during the cooling-down ceremony. You point weakly over across the gorge.

"Be careful!" you warn. "We need backup, for the fire."

Finn turns to Brouillard.

"I didn't realize it was this bad," he says. "Maybe there's a concussion."

Confused, you look out to where you are pointing. The trees glisten, green and whole. Nothing is charred or smoking, as if no fire ever took place. Stamos laughs and gives you a small kick in the leg.

"You'll be fine," he says, "I think we just need to get you back to camp. You've just been dreaming here all day."

You get into the helicopter with the others. As you leave, you see the elk walk slowly by.

The End

Your radio takes a few tries to work properly, and then you get Stamos on the line.

"Stamos," you say. "I've had a report that there's an enormous fire on Trillion Gorge."

"Unclear," Stamos answers. "Please repeat."

"Large forest fire," you insist, "Location Trillion Gorge."

"Kid," says Stamos. "There is no place anywhere near here named Trillion Gorge. Can you give me your coordinates?"

You look up and realize Nascha is nowhere to be seen; she's completely disappeared.

"Coordinates?" you repeat weakly.

"I'm going to radio a copter to pick you up," Stamos says. "Stay within radio distance. I think you're overtired."

You sit on a boulder. Maybe Stamos is right. You look out across the canyons and watch the sun sink beyond the horizon, oranges and yellows spreading across the sky. You close your eyes for a second, turn up your radio, and lean back to wait. It's been a long day out here in the wild. Was Nascha just a ghost?

The End

As you begin to climb, you hear the sound of a helicopter overhead and look up with relief. Brouillard looks down at you anxiously, and they direct the copter close enough that you and Finn can be picked up.

"Get in!" shouts Brouillard. He and Stamos lift you off the side of the ridge and into the helicopter. "We haven't spotted the people you saw yet," Brouillard tells you. "And that's not a good sign. We have a report from another ranger station that there was a family of three people who last checked in three days ago. They're filming a nature documentary and had limited supplies. They were probably already lost when the fire broke out."

Brouillard gives you and Finn a serious look.

"Look out at that smoke," he says. Over about an acre of fast-burning trees, a column of smoke is building vertically, capped with a short, thick layer of cloud. "This is a plume fire," Brouillard tells you gravely. "The heat of the fire is sucking air into a thermal. It's going to be unpredictable and very dangerous. I need your full attention and focus."

Turn to page 94.

You and Finn don't say anything, just nod your heads and watch as the copter looms closer and closer to the fire. There are three people to be rescued, so you, Brouillard, and Finn will all be needed. Stamos will drop down and work on the fire with rangers who are headed over to meet him. Just like during the trial run, you stand in your static line, ready to plunge into the fire. You give Finn a quick smile just before you jump and wish him good luck.

The rangers on the ground radio that they have located the family. Brouillard rushes through preparations before the jump, anxious to reach them. You and Finn don't even speak, you're so focused.

Surprisingly, the jump goes smoothly. All three members of the documentary team are rescued. When you're brought back to camp, they are so inspired (and have lost so much of their previous footage) that they decide to follow you and Finn for a year, making a documentary called *Smoke Jumpers: Kings of the Sky*. You and Finn will become semi-famous and will have to turn down several television talk show appearances, claiming you'd rather be jumping than achieving celebrity status.

The End

"The police. That's it. I'll just call the police. Why didn't I do that before?" you say to yourself out loud. There are telephones in the office, as well as on the wall of the mess hall. The mess hall is the easiest to get to.

Moments later you are there, lifting the receiver and dialing. "Operator, I need—hey, what's with this thing?" The line is dead. You slam the phone back on the hook. Heart pounding, you race to the office. The door is locked. Without hesitating, you grab a rock, smash the window, and reach in to unlock the door. The phone there is dead, too.

Frantically you search for the radio phones. When you find the rack where they are stored, you're not surprised to find them gone. You wonder what to do now.

As you stand there, wondering what to do next, several options come to you. You can either run back to the tents and wake the others, return to Erica and see what you can do, or grab a vehicle and drive to the police for help. All these plans sound good, but they're all equally risky, too.

*If you decide to wake the others,
turn to page 97.*

*If you return to Erica at the parachute shed,
turn to page 98.*

*If you decide to take a vehicle and get the
police, turn to page 81.*

The engine, as if in agony, groans and coughs. You turn the key again and listen to it growl and sputter. Then it catches, erupting into its full, impressive sound.

"Okay! Let's get rolling!" you shout, psyching yourself up.

The gearshift is on the floor. It takes you a while to locate reverse, but when you do, the big truck jerks into action, moving backward and almost clipping one of the 4X4s.

Moments later you're rolling down the dirt road, out of the camp, and picking up speed. As soon as you are clear of the camp, you switch on the lights.

"Now where do I go?" you say, addressing the space around you. "I don't know where the police are, I don't even know where anything is."

Turn to page 103.

You reason that there is security in numbers, so you decide to get the others involved. The tents are spread out in the area surrounding the cabins. Some are in the woods, others near the small lake. In the dark with the moon covered by heavy clouds, you find it hard to locate all of them.

"Hey, wake up. We need help. Keep your voice down," you whisper at each tent. Some wake easily, others are really hard to rouse. Soon you have them all in a group in the woods.

"This is the deal. Intruders have entered camp. Finn and I found them sabotaging our gear. Erica is keeping an eye on them over by the parachute shed. They have taken Finn hostage."

All at once there is a flurry of conversation, some concerned, some playfully skeptical. The only emergency for most of them is that they're losing sleep and wish to get back to their tents.

The babble is irritating, but you try to be patient. Time is slipping by, and Finn's life is in danger. *Why can't these people get it together?* you ask yourself.

"Okay, listen up! Those who want to help, over here." You motion to your side. "Those who don't, go back to your tents. But I'm telling you, this is no joke."

Suddenly the seriousness in your voice catches hold, and everyone shuts up.

Turn to page 106.

There's no time to wake the others or get to the police, you decide. Running at full tilt, you return to the parachute shed.

"Erica. Hey, it's me," you whisper.

"She's in here, kid. I suggest you come in."

As if in a dream, you cross the open area and mount the steps of the porch. Common sense tells you to run away as fast as you can go, but you stay where you are. Jumping out of the plane was a cinch compared to this.

The door opens slowly, revealing a short, paunchy man with a snub-nosed revolver. "Be my guest, please," he says, motioning you inside. This whole scene smacks of some low-grade television drama—guns, hostages—it all seems so crazy. Nothing makes sense. Your world has suddenly gone topsy-turvy.

You reach down inside yourself for strength and calmness to continue. It's a pretty far reach, and all that you come up with is a lot more fear.

Inside, you find Erica and Finn sitting in chairs, their hands bound behind them. The man with the gun is next to them, a smile on his face. He looks to be in his mid-forties and is dressed in a camouflage outfit, the type you buy in army-navy surplus stores. He has streaks of black greasepaint over his face and is wearing gloves and a bandana around his forehead.

Turn to page 101.

"This is all going to be very easy," the man announces. "We're going to wait until dawn. Your friends are going to get up as usual. Erica here will tell them it's jump time. You will join them. Once inside the plane—"

He doesn't have a chance to finish his sentence—Dot bursts through the door and charges the man. She picks him up over her head and sends him crashing to the floor like a pro wrestler. Dropping to her knees she takes rawhide bootlaces and has him tied up like a rodeo heifer calf in seconds.

"Dot, what happened?" you blurt out, stunned by the sudden turn of events.

These bozos are some kind of hired mercenaries," she says. "Their sick deal is environmental sabotage. They'll threaten to burn forests or poison water supplies if the community or government doesn't pay. It's extortion, plain and simple."

Turn to page 110.

Following your instincts, you head onto the paved two-lane road and drive until you come upon the first house, almost eleven miles away.

A grumpy man answers the door; but once you explain to him what is going on, he seems to wake up and is anxious to help.

He telephones the police, and they order you to stay where you are so no one gets hurt. All you can do now is wait.

Twenty minutes later you hear the unmistakable sound of helicopters. You can't restrain yourself any longer. You thank the man for his kindness and help, and soon you are back in the truck, heading for the camp.

Unfortunately, about five miles from the camp, your truck sputters and rolls to a halt. You don't know what the problem is, and you don't have time to figure it out. One thing's for sure, you're on your feet now.

Turn to the next page.

It's bound to take you almost an hour to cover the five miles. You run as fast as you can, but by the time you finally make it to the camp, everything is over and the police are wrapping things up. Finn fills you in on what happened.

"They call themselves environmental commandos," he says. "They threaten to destroy forests unless they're paid a ransom. These guys are nuts."

"Yeah, but they almost got away with it," you reply.

The image of blazing forests and frightened hostages fills your mind. This has been enough for you for one day. It's time to get some sleep.

The End

"I need two of you to go for the police," you tell the group. "The phones are out. Dot and the others aren't around. I don't know where they are, but right now I don't really care as long as they're out."

"What do you mean by that?" a girl named Sally asks.

You are on the spot. "I can't find them. They must have the night off, or—who knows."

"No way!" Sally shouts. "You aren't going to tell me that you think they're in on this. If you are, then this must be a joke."

"Maybe that's the way they celebrate our first jump, you know, with some kind of crazy joke," someone else says.

"Maybe this is some kind of test," suggests another.

Several others murmur with agreement.

"Then it doesn't matter. Two of you go for the police. Take one of the cars in the motor pool. The others come with me. Keep quiet and spread out. We'll surround the cabin."

Go on to the next page.

Two people fade off toward the motor pool areas as you and the others move toward the parachute shed. The flashlight there has gone off, and all is quiet. Moments later you are back at the spot where you last saw Erica, now nowhere to be found.

The darkness that surrounds you is overwhelming. Everything seems so quiet and calm, you half expect that if you went back to Finn's tent, he would be inside, safe and sleeping.

"So, whassup? I don't see nothin'," says a boy called Mick with a strong Bronx accent.

"I don't know. But let's find out," you say, edging out from the cover of the woods and moving toward the parachute shed.

Turn to the next page.

Suddenly there is a coughing, sputtering sound. Then it catches and turns into a hammering, throaty roar as it rips through the darkness.

"It's the plane! They're in the plane!" someone yells.

The number two engine turns over, stammers a bit, and then falls into its rhythm. The landing lights come on, and you can both see and hear the big plane taxiing down the strip, positioning itself into the wind for takeoff.

Then a voice comes from a radio inside the parachute shed. "We have a full load of hostages. I repeat. We have a full load of hostages."

You dash into the shed. There you find the radio phone sitting on a packing table, squawking out the message.

"What are your demands?" you ask, keying the transmit button.

There is a moment of scratchy noise and then the voice comes back, "Very simple. We want you to set fire to the camp."

"You must be joking," you say back incredulously at the enormity and the stupidity of the demand.

"Maybe you would rather talk to the one called Erica?"

Erica's voice comes over the radio. It is thin and reflects great tension and fear.

Turn to page 111.

110

The sound of several helicopters interrupts Dot. You watch as two state police choppers land outside the shed and Brouillard steps off.

"We radioed them from the plane," Dot says, grinning ear to ear.

Brouillard and the police take over. With dawn not too far away, everyone finally returns to their tents.

"There'll be no jump this morning," Brouillard announces. "But be ready tomorrow."

Right now jumping is the farthest thing from your mind. All you can do as you climb into bed is think about sleep and the peace that it brings.

The End

"He's not kidding," Erica says. "We're in the plane. Our hands are tied, and we're on the static line without parachutes. There are three of them with us plus the pilot."

"What about Dot, Finn, and the others?" you query.

"Roger for all of them. They were already in the plane when we got here."

"Who are these people?" you ask.

"That's all the time you get," a hard voice replies. "Who we are is of no concern to you. We have a job to do, and you are going to help us. Your payment is the safe return of your friends. Failure to comply will result in their release one by one over the drop zone."

You hear the big DC-3 overhead making a large circle, its motors pulling it through the cloud cover. Moments dangle with painful intensity.

"The green light is going on. They're preparing us to jump," comes a panicked voice.

"Okay, okay! We'll do it! Wait!"

Turn to the next page.

Sick with fear, you and the others fan out and put match to paper, pine needles, and brush. The flames are greedy. You watch as the entire camp burns to the ground. Overhead, the engines of the Otter grow fainter and fainter as the plane heads north in the direction of Canada.

Weeks later the wreckage of the Otter is found high in the Canadian Rockies. There are no survivors.

The End

You hear the sound of footsteps coming toward you. Although you want to escape, your body won't move. It is as if you've become a part of the earth, something silent and immobile.

The flashlight shines right into your face. As you shield your eyes, you are pulled roughly to your feet, slapped several times, and pushed violently inside the parachute shed along with Finn.

Minutes later flames hungrily consume the dry old wood. Your training has told you to stay low. You put your shirt over your mouth and nose; you know it's the smoke that will get you before the flames. The near wall collapses in a shower of sparks and flames, just missing you.

You see the collapsed wall as your last chance as visibility in the acrid smoke drops to near zero. You dash through the ring of fire, clear a burning beam, and sprint out into the night. You collapse onto the cool grass, coughing wildly. You know you've been burned on parts of your body, but the good news is you hear someone nearby coughing—Finn. So now it's your turn to be medivaced out to a top burn unit at University Hospital. You feel glad to be alive. You acquitted yourself well as a smoke jumper. By the time the helicopter lands, even though you're in shock, you are dreaming of coming back next year.

The End

116

"So, big deal," you say. "A couple of strangers. They're probably just friends of Brouillard."

"No, they weren't friends of anyone here. They were messing around with our equipment," Finn says.

"What do you mean? Were they stealing?"

"Worse—sabotage. At least that's what I think they were doing. I first saw them out by the plane. They were messing around inside. I couldn't tell exactly what was going on. There were no lights, but I heard a lot of whispering."

"Then what?"

"They—" Finn suddenly peers around the tent and squints into the dark. "Hey, I think they're in the parachute shed."

"Let's get Erica!" you say.

"No, let's find out what they're up to first and track them back to their vehicle."

It's a hard decision. Caution dictates going to Erica for help; action says to follow these people before they get away.

"Are you coming with me?" Finn asks.

If you decide to go for Erica, turn to page 75.

If you decide to stay with Finn and investigate, turn to page 55.

CREDITS

Illustrator: Laurence Peguy was born and raised in les Landes, one of the most beautiful regions of France. She received her Baccalaureate in 1997 in Literature, attended the Visual Art Institute of Orleans, and graduated from The Emile Cohl School of Animation in 2002. She has worked as a cartoon portraitist at Epcot Center at Disneyworld, Florida. She currently works for the French creative group "2 Minutes" as a Flash animator. Laurence also illustrated *The Abominable Snowman, Choose Your Own Adventure #1.*

Cover Artist: Wes Louie was born and raised in Los Angeles, where he grew up drawing. He attended Pasadena City College, where he made a lot of great friends and contacts, and then the Art Center. Wes majored in illustration, but also took classes in industrial design and entertainment. He has been working in the entertainment industry since 1998 in a variety of fields.

This book was brought to life by a great group of people:

Shannon Gilligan, Publisher

Melissa Bounty, Senior Editor

Stacey Boyd, Designer

Nina Jaffe, Proofreader

ABOUT THE AUTHOR

R. A. MONTGOMERY has hiked in the Himalayas, climbed mountains in Europe, scuba-dived in Central America, and worked in Africa. He lives in France in the winter, travels frequently to Asia, and calls Vermont home. Montgomery graduated from Williams College and attended graduate school at Yale University and NYU. His interests include macroeconomics, geopolitics, mythology, history, mystery novels, and music. He has two grown sons, a daughter-in-law, and two granddaughters. His wife, Shannon Gilligan, is an author and noted interactive game designer. Montgomery feels that the generation of people under 15 is the most important asset in our world.

Visit us online at CYOA.com for games and other fun stuff, or to write to R. A. Montgomery!